**Welcome to ALADDIN QUIX!**

If you are looking for fast, fun-to-read stories with colorful characters, lots of kid-friendly humor, easy-to-follow action, entertaining story lines, and lively illustrations, then **ALADDIN QUIX** is for you!

But wait, there's more!

If you're also looking for stories with tables of contents; word lists; about-the-book questions; 64, 80, or 96 pages; short chapters; short paragraphs; and large fonts, then **ALADDIN QUIX** is *definitely* for you!

**ALADDIN QUIX:** The next step between ready to reads and longer, more challenging chapter books, for readers five to eight years old.

# A Miss Mallard Mystery

# TAXI TO INTRIGUE

## ROBERT QUACKENBUSH

### ALADDIN QUIX

New York  London  Toronto  Sydney  New Delhi

ALADDIN QUIX

Simon & Schuster Children's Publishing Division

1230 Avenue of the Americas, New York, New York 10020

This Aladdin QUIX hardcover edition May 2019

Copyright © 1984 by Robert Quackenbush

Also available in an Aladdin QUIX paperback edition.

All rights reserved, including the right of reproduction in whole or in part in any form.

ALADDIN and the related marks and colophon are trademarks of Simon & Schuster, Inc.

For information about special discounts for bulk purchases, please contact Simon & Schuster Special Sales at 1-866-506-1949 or business@simonandschuster.com.

The Simon & Schuster Speakers Bureau can bring authors to your live event. For more information or to book an event contact the Simon & Schuster Speakers Bureau at 1-866-248-3049 or visit our website at www.simonspeakers.com.

Designed by Tiara Iandiorio

The illustrations for this book were rendered in pen and ink and wash.

The text of this book was set in Archer Medium.

Manufactured in the United States of America 0419 FFG

2 4 6 8 10 9 7 5 3 1

Library of Congress Control Number 2018959536

ISBN 978-1-5344-1412-9 (hc)

ISBN 978-1-5344-1411-2 (pbk)

ISBN 978-1-5344-1413-6 (eBook)

First for Piet and Margie,

and now for Emma and Aidan

# Cast of Characters

**Miss Mallard:** World-famous ducktective

**taxi driver:** Driver who takes Miss Mallard all over London

**Winston and Christopher:** Owners of the Winston & Christopher Pastry Shop

**Archibald Dusty Duck:** Set designer at Madame Tufflebottom's Waxworks

**Reginald P. Tree Duck:** Guard at the Tower of London

**Wallace Pochard:** Clock repairman at Big Ben

**Inspector Lynas T. Eider:** Member of London's police force

# What's in Miss Mallard's Bag?

Miss Mallard has many detective tools she brings with her on her adventures around the world.

In her knitting bag she usually has:

- Newspaper clippings
- Knitting needles and yarn
- A magnifying glass
- A flashlight
- A mirror
- A travel guide
- Chocolates for her nephew

# Contents

# Contents

# 1

## Shopping in London

**Miss Mallard**, the world famous ducktective, left her home in the country to shop in London. Upon arriving, she hailed a taxi.

"Piccadilly Circus," she said to the driver. "I like to shop there."

Just as she was climbing into the taxi, someone ran up and handed her a box.

**"Here, take this!"** said the mysterious stranger.

At the same time a **shrill** police whistle was heard. In a flash the stranger had disappeared into the crowd.

**"Good heavens!"** said Miss Mallard. "What was that about?"

Miss Mallard sat down in the taxi and looked at the box. The address on the lid said:

WINSTON & CHRISTOPHER

PASTRY SHOP

25 Shepard's Court SW1, London

Inside the box was a beautiful cake. A message was written in script across the top:

*Happy Birthday Milly!*

"What a pity," said Miss Mallard. "Someone is without a birthday cake. I must look into this. A new case is about to begin!"

◀ 4 ▶

# 2

## Many Millys

"I've changed my mind," said Miss Mallard to the **taxi driver**. "I can go to Piccadilly Circus another time. Please take me to the Winston and Christopher Pastry Shop. It is at 25 Shepard's Court."

Then she exclaimed, **"And make it fast!"**

"As you wish, ma'am," said the driver.

He sped through the fog to the pastry shop. It didn't take long to reach their destination. But the cobblestone streets made it a bumpy ride.

Miss Mallard thanked the driver and paid the fare.

She stepped out of the taxi into the fog and looked over her shoulder.

Her quick eyes flashed on an odd-looking duck standing on a nearby street corner. He was reading a newspaper, but Miss Mallard was sure he was watching her at the same time. She hurried into the shop.

Miss Mallard introduced herself to **Winston and Christopher**, the shop's owners. They were busy decorating cakes. She told them she wanted to find out who had bought the birthday cake that had mysteriously been given to her.

"*I'll* look this up," Winston said to Christopher. "*You* have a lot of catching up to do this morning."

Winston finished printing the words "Happy Anniversary" on a cake. Then he went to the counter and took a stack of orders from a **spindle**. He went through them and removed three orders.

"Here are three orders for birthday cakes with the name Milly on them," said Winston. "They were ordered by **Archibald Dusty Duck, Reginald P. Tree Duck**, and

**Wallace Pochard**. We have their addresses, but not their phone numbers. Here is a telephone book to look them up."

He handed the orders and the phone book to Miss Mallard. Then he glanced at his partner. Christopher was writing a name in script across the top of a huge birthday cake.

**"No! No! No!"** shouted Winston. "The name on that cake is to be Daphne—not Ophelia!"

Christopher grumbled, scraped

off the icing, and began writing again with his pastry tube.

Miss Mallard **leafed** through the telephone book and then handed it back to Winston.

"None of the names are listed in the book," she said. "But I've copied down the names and addresses from the orders. I think I'll go on a mission and find the owner of this birthday cake. I want to solve the mystery."

"What a nice thing to do," said Winston. **"Good luck!"**

He turned to Christopher and said, "**No! No! No!** Daphne is not with an *f.* What's the matter with you today?"

Miss Mallard tucked the cake box into her knitting bag. As she left the shop, Winston and Christopher were arguing loudly.

Out on the street, she **peered** through the fog. The duck on the street corner was still there.

*Why is he spying on me?* she wondered.

# 3

## Almond Aroma

Miss Mallard hailed another taxi. She told the driver to take her to the first address on her list. The taxi raced through traffic and pulled up in front of Madame Tufflebottom's Waxworks.

"**Hmmmm,**" said Miss Mallard to herself. "No wonder the name Archibald Dusty Duck was not listed in the phone book at this address. He doesn't *live* here. He must work here."

Miss Mallard paid the driver and went inside the museum. She asked to see Archibald Dusty Duck. The manager told her that Archibald was a set designer and pointed the way to his office.

Miss Mallard walked through room after room of wax figures.

Finally, she came to a room called the Chamber of Horrors. She shuddered at all the frightening figures she saw.

Archibald's office was on the other side.

Suddenly she smelled the **aroma** of almonds. Someone grabbed her knitting bag and at the same time gave her a strong push.

Miss Mallard pulled her bag away from whoever had tried to grab it, but—**ooof!**—she lost her balance.

Before she knew what was happening, she tumbled into an **iron maiden**. She was locked inside! She quacked loudly for help,

**"HELP!**

**"HELP!**

**"Can anybody hear me?"**

Archibald Dusty Duck himself heard Miss Mallard quacking for help. He quickly came to her rescue and asked, **"How did you wind up in here?"**

He took her into his office and poured her a cup of tea.

While Miss Mallard sipped her tea and tried to figure out who had pushed her, she remembered the cake.

She took it out of her knitting bag and asked Archibald if it belonged to him.

**"Why, no!"** said Archibald as he pointed to an empty box on the windowsill. "That is mine. Or what is left of it. It was for Milly, who works here. We celebrated her birthday today."

"Then I shall have to go on to

the next person and place on my list," said Miss Mallard.

She finished her tea, and after thanking Archibald Dusty Duck for rescuing her, she left the wax museum. Outside she caught a **glimpse** of the duck peering at her over a newspaper.

Quickly she hailed another taxi to take her to the next address. It was the Tower of London.

When she arrived, Miss Mallard asked a guard where she could find Reginald P. Tree Duck.

She was told that he was also a guard and that his **post** was at the top of the central keep, the White Tower.

Miss Mallard began walking up the stairs inside the tower one step at a time. It was a slow, steep climb to the top.

Suddenly she was aware of the aroma of almonds, which she had smelled at the wax museum.

"How odd," she said to herself.

At the same time she heard a loud . . .

# CRASH!

# BANG!

# BOOM!

# 4

## Over a Barrel

A heavy barrel came rolling down the stairs! It was aiming straight at her! In a flash, Miss Mallard dove into a **niche** in the wall next to the stairs.

She was saved in the nick of

time from the crashing barrel!

It landed at the bottom of the stairs. Guards came rushing to Miss Mallard to see if she was all right. They took her to their room and poured her a cup of tea.

The guards were very puzzled about the barrel and wondered how it had gotten on the stairs. Miss Mallard wasn't puzzled—she was sure that someone was out to get her. **But who? And why?**

Reginald P. Tree Duck, the second name on her list, was among

the guards. Miss Mallard asked him if the cake she had safely brought in her knitting bag was his.

"No," said Reginald. "I have mine in my locker downstairs. It's for my sister Milly. It's her birthday today, and I'm taking the cake to a party at her house."

When Miss Mallard finished her tea, she asked Reginald to call a taxi.

As she rode to the last address on her list, she looked out the rear window to see if she was being followed. Sure enough, in the taxi right behind hers sat the duck who had been spying on her.

**"Lose that taxi behind us!"** Miss Mallard said to her driver.

"Right away!" said the driver.

With that, he stepped on the gas pedal and picked up speed.

# 5

## Double Trouble

The driver **swerved** the taxi into foggy side streets and down dim alleys until he was sure the taxi behind them was out of sight.

"Now take me to Big Ben," said Miss Mallard. Her driver

sped to London's great clock.

"Thank you!" said Miss Mallard to the driver as she paid her fare.

Then she got out of the taxi and went to the entrance of Big Ben's tower.

A guard there told her that Wallace Pochard, the last person on her list, was a clock repairman. He was at work cleaning Big Ben.

Miss Mallard climbed the stairs to the top of the tower. Once again, it was a slow, steep climb to the top.

When she got there, only the whistle of the wind and the **tick-tock** of the giant clock could be heard.

"Wallace Pochard?" called Miss Mallard.

She called his name again, this time louder. There was no answer.

Suddenly Miss Mallard smelled the aroma of almonds. At the same time, she felt herself being pushed from behind. She went falling through an open window in the face of the clock!

# 6

## Just in Time

With her only free wing—for she clutched her knitting bag securely with the other—she grabbed one of the giant clock hands. Holding it tightly, she wondered how long she could hang on.

Just as she felt her wing slipping, someone grasped her firmly and pulled her back into the tower to safety. Through dazed eyes, Miss Mallard looked to see who had saved her. It was the duck who had been following her.

**"Who are you?"** asked Miss Mallard.

"I am **Inspector Lynas T. Eider** from London's police force. And with me is Wallace Pochard."

"Have a cup of tea from my **thermos**, miss," said Wallace.

"You've had quite a fright."

Miss Mallard took the tea and asked, "Who pushed me?"

"Not I," said the inspector. "Nor was it Wallace Pochard. He took me to you when he saw you hanging from the clock hand. **Whoever did it got away!**"

# 7

## Ducky Wucky

Miss Mallard took the cake from her knitting bag and asked Wallace if it belonged to him. Wallace said that he already had one like it in his lunch basket for his wife, Milly.

"May I see that cake?" asked the inspector.

Miss Mallard handed it to him. She watched in horror as he crumbled it to bits.

He pulled a tiny **capsule** from the pile of crumbs. He opened the capsule and removed rolls of tiny paper.

"So *that's* why you have been following me!" exclaimed Miss Mallard.

"Yes," said the inspector. "I hoped you would lead me to the

head of a spy ring. These are plans for a secret weapon—**the Ducky Wucky walkie-talkie!**

"Someone was trying to get them out of the country and into enemy hands," he added. "I caught the spy who tossed the cake to you when he saw the jig was up. But he's not talking. We may never find out who was supposed to receive this cake."

Miss Mallard sniffed the air. Then she took a bite of the crumbled cake. It tasted of almonds.

"**Aha!**" she cried. "**Spies! Secret plans!** And now that I've put all the clues together, I know who the ringleader of the operation is. I'll take you to him right now."

They rushed by taxi to the pastry shop and burst inside. Winston and Christopher were startled.

"What is it?" asked Winston.

"One of you is guilty of being an enemy agent," said Inspector Eider. "And Miss Mallard here has the evidence against you."

**"Impossible,"** said Winston. "I would never do such a thing. I'm much too busy with my cakes."

"That's true," said Miss Mallard. "But I can't say the same for your partner, Christopher."

Christopher **darted** for the back door. Quickly Miss Mallard **heaved** a tray of cream puffs at him. He slipped on them and landed in a vat of chocolate sauce!

# 8

## The Triumph

**"Jolly good work, Miss Mallard!"** said the inspector as they all gathered around the vat. "But how did you know Christopher was the leader of the ring?"

"Easy," said Miss Mallard. "The

cake was not meant for delivery
to anyone but the person you
have already arrested. He is the
**go-between** for the enemy."

"But where does Christopher
fit into all of this?" asked the
inspector.

"He obtained the plans, and
probably other plans as well," said
Miss Mallard. "He has been let-
ting them leak out of the country
in his cakes."

She paused and then added,
"I'll bet if you ask Winston, you

will find that Christopher was in and out of the shop all day. He was trying to get back the evidence. He had that on his mind from the moment I walked into the shop with the cake."

"I still can't figure out how you suspected Christopher," said the inspector.

"Well," said Miss Mallard, "the moment I tasted the cake I knew it had almond flavoring. I had smelled almonds each time my life was in danger. That's how I knew either Winston or Christopher, with the scent of almond flavoring on their clothes, had followed me."

The inspector nodded, and Miss Mallard explained, "Then I remembered Christopher decorates his cakes with script writing—like he did on the evidence—and Winston *prints* his cake messages. So I knew who was guilty."

With that, Winston reached for a birthday cake and promptly crowned Christopher with it.

Inspector Eider turned to Miss

Mallard and said, "Miss Mallard, England thanks you. And I thank you. May I take you out for a cup of tea after I deliver this crook to prison?"

"Oh, dear," said Miss Mallard. "I've had so much tea today that I'm beginning to feel like a **soggy** tea bag. But I wouldn't mind sharing a cake with you. As long as it isn't almond-flavored. That would be very nice."

# Word List

**aroma (uh·RO·muh):** A pleasant smell

**capsule (CAP·sul):** A small container

**darted (DAR·ted):** Quickly moved from one place to another

**glimpse (GLIMPS):** A short look at something

**go-between (GO-bee·tween):** Someone who takes messages from one person to another

**heaved (HEEVD):** Threw with great effort

**iron maiden (EYE·urn MAY·den):** A hollow metal statue

**leafed (LEEFD):** Turned the pages

**niche (NEESH):** A curved space in a wall

**peered (PEERD):** Looked closely and carefully

**post (POHST):** The place where a guard stands

**shrill (SHRIL):** Having a high-pitched sound

**soggy (SOG·ee):** Very wet and usually soft

**spindle (SPIN·dul):** A thin rod or stick with pointed ends

**swerved (SWERVD):** Changed direction suddenly

**thermos (THUR·mus):** A container that keeps liquids cold or hot for long periods of time

# Questions

1. How many birthday cakes did Winston and Christopher bake for Milly?

2. Did you suspect Christopher of being the secret agent?

3. Why was the odd-looking duck following Miss Mallard?

4. What places in London did Miss Mallard investigate?

5. What did Miss Mallard keep smelling?

# Acknowledgments

My thanks and appreciation go to Jon Anderson, president and publisher of Simon & Schuster Children's Books, and his talented team: Karen Nagel, executive editor; Karin Paprocki, art director; Tiara Iandiorio, designer; Elizabeth Mims, managing editor; Sara Berko, production manager; Tricia Lin, assistant editor; and Richard Ackoon, executive coordinator; for launching out into the world again these incredible new editions of my Miss Mallard Mystery books for today's young readers everywhere.

# CHUCKLE YOUR WAY THROUGH THESE EASY-TO-READ ILLUSTRATED CHAPTER BOOKS!

EXTRAORDINARY WARREN
A SUPER CHICKEN
by SARAH DILLARD

EXTRAORDINARY WARREN SAVES THE DAY
by SARAH DILLARD

SNAIL HAS LUNCH
MARY PETERSON

BUCK'S TOOTH
Diane Kredensor

THIS LITTLE PIGGY
AN OWNER'S MANUAL
Cynd Mc